This Little Tiger book belongs to:

_____

_____

_____

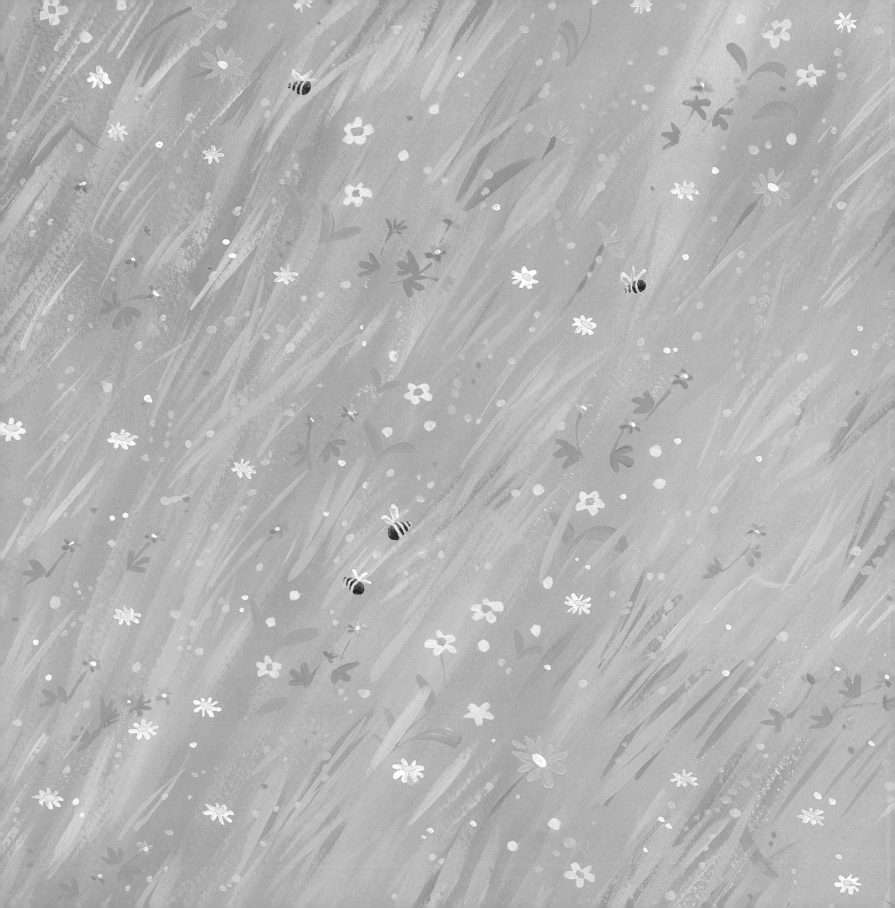

In memory of my Dad ~ C F

For Isaac and Daniel ~ J C

LITTLE TIGER PRESS
1 The Coda Centre, 189 Munster Road, London SW6 6AW
www.littletiger.co.uk

First published in Great Britain 2009
This edition published 2016

Text copyright © Claire Freedman 2009
Illustrations copyright © Jane Chapman 2009
Visit Jane Chapman at www.ChapmanandWarnes.com
Claire Freedman and Jane Chapman have asserted
their rights to be identified as the author and illustrator of
this work under the Copyright, Designs and Patents Act, 1988

ISBN 978-1-84869-460-6
Printed in China
LTP/1900/1573/0616

2 4 6 8 10 9 7 5 3 1

When We're Together

Claire Freedman   Jane Chapman

LITTLE TIGER PRESS

London

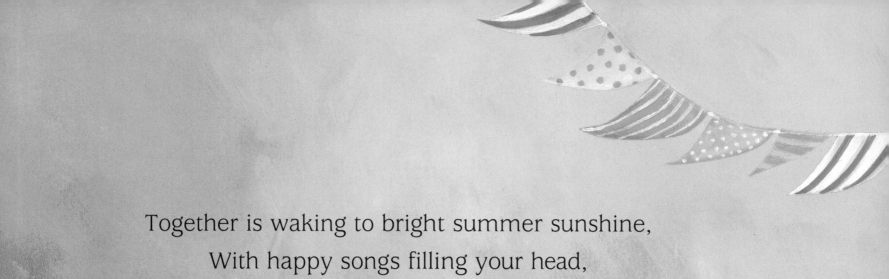

Together is waking to bright summer sunshine,
With happy songs filling your head,
It's singing the words at the top of your voice
As you bounce up and down on your bed.

Being together is running down hillsides,
So fast that you almost can't stop!
Together is landing in one giant heap,
And catching your breath as you flop.

Together's the fun that you have when it's snowing,
The sledges you can't wait to ride,
It's giggling while trying to hold up each other
Whenever your feet slip and slide!

Being together is having a secret
You share with your very best friend,
It's talking and listening and laughing together,
And knowing your friendship won't end.

Time spent together is getting all messy,
It's squidgy mud pies that you pat,
It's squashing and squelching
and stamping them down,
And hearing the sound as they splat!

Together is riding on Daddy's
strong shoulders,
And feeling as tall as a tree,
It's going exploring and having adventures,
And sharing new things that you see.

Together is kicking through leaves,
crisp and crunchy,
And watching them swirl through the air,
It's leaping in drifts that come up to your knees,
And showering the leaves everywhere.

Being together is fireside cuddles,
It's magical stories we share,
It's hearing the rain pitter-pat on the windows,
Squish-squashed in our favourite chair.

Together is searching in seaweedy rock pools,
Then catching a crab in your hand,
It's squealing as cold waves rush over your feet,
And wiggling your toes in the sand.

Sometimes together is just being quiet,
Like gazing at clouds in the sky,
It's seeing the shapes and the patterns they make,
And counting them as they float by.

Together is pillow fights all round your bedroom,
And giggling and running to hide,
It's white fluffy feathers that fly through the air
So it looks like it's snowing inside.

Time spent together is big hugs at bedtime,
And being tucked in snug and tight,
It's sweet dreams and moonbeams
and drowsy eyes closing,
And sleeping safe all through the night.

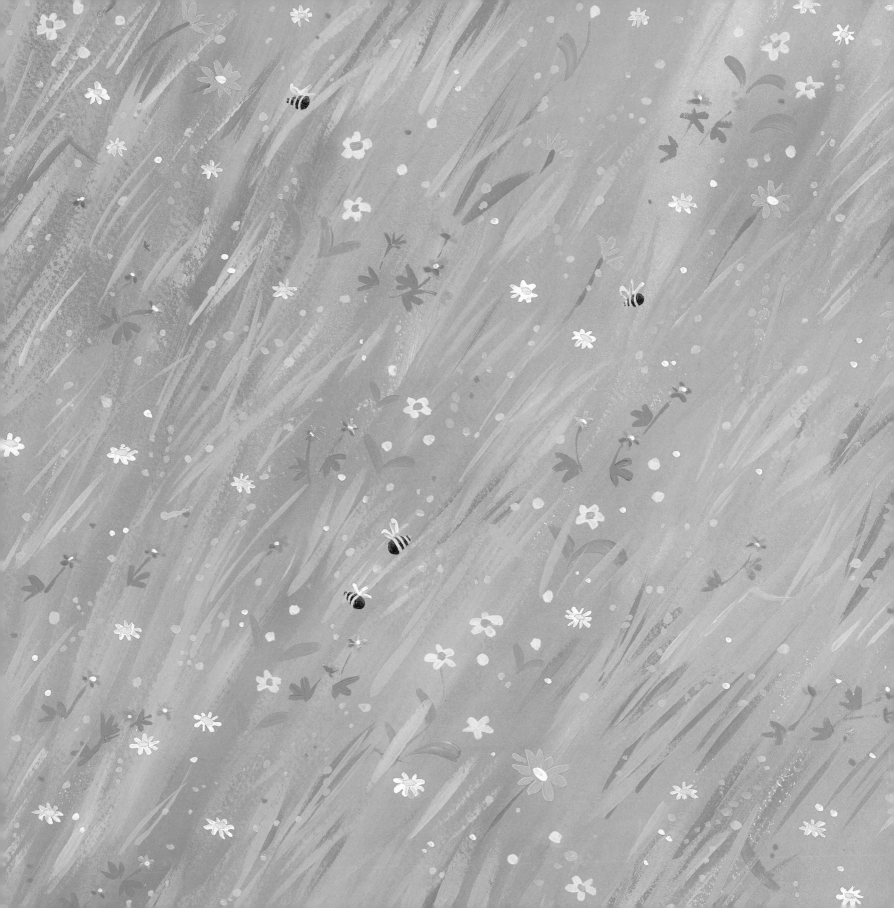